LOUIS PASTEUR

PEOPLE WHO MADE A DIFFERENCE

David and Patricia Armentrout

Rourke Publishing LLC
Vero Beach, Florida 32964

© 2002 Rourke Publishing LLC

PHOTO CREDITS:
Photos provided by the National Library of Medicine, Bethesda, MD

EDITORIAL SERVICES:
Pamela Schroeder

Library of Congress Cataloging-in-Publication Data

Armentrout, David, 1962-
    Louis Pasteur / David & Patricia Armentrout
        p. cm. — (People who made a difference)
    Includes index.
    ISBN 1-58952-056-4
    1. Pasteur, Louis, 1822-1895—Juvenile literature.
    2. Scientists—France—Biography—Juvenile literature. 3. Microbiologists—France—Biography—Juvenile literature. [1. Pasteur, Louis, 1822-1895.
    2. Microbiologist. 3. Scientists] I. Armentrout, Patricia, 1960-II. Title.

Q143.P2 A76 2001
579'.092—dc21
[B]
                                                                2001018584

Printed in the USA

TABLE OF CONTENTS

YOUNG LOUIS PASTEUR

Louis Pasteur was born in France in 1822. As a child, Louis enjoyed drawing and painting. However, as a teenager he wanted to teach science.

Louis went to school in Paris. There he met Jean-Baptiste Dumas, a chemistry teacher.

Louis liked Dumas. He became more excited about science. In 1847, Louis earned his doctor of science degree.

Louis Pasteur spent his life helping others.

CRYSTALS

Louis Pasteur was very interested in how things grew. Pasteur studied salt crystals. He wanted to see how they were made. When light shines through some crystals, the light beam bends. Pasteur wondered why.

After months of studying, Pasteur discovered why some crystals bend light and others do not. His discovery was a great step forward in science.

Pasteur at work in his science lab

THE PASTEUR FAMILY

Louis Pasteur taught science at the University of Strasbourg in 1849. There he met Marie Laurent. They married that year. They had three daughters and one son by 1863.

Marie supported Louis and his scientific studies. She even helped him with his work.

MICROBES

In 1856, a man who made alcohol from beet juice needed Pasteur's help. Some of the juice went sour. The man did not know why.

Pasteur studied the beet juice under a microscope. He saw tiny living cells, called **microbes**, in both juices. The good juice had **yeast** microbes. Yeast helps make alcohol. The sour juice had microbes called germs.

Pasteur often used animals in his scientific studies.

PASTEURIZATION

Pasteur did many experiments. He found that heat could kill germs. Today, everyone uses heat to kill germs. This process is called **pasteurization**.

Pasteur kept studying germ microbes. He discovered that germs could be found in the air. He found that some germs could cause disease.

Scientists study microbes and diseases at the Pasteur Institute.

DISEASE AND FAMILY TRAGEDY

Diseases were spreading across cities in France. Many people died including Pasteur's three daughters. Pasteur, and other scientists, worked hard to find a way to stop the disease.

In 1868, Pasteur had a stroke. It left him paralyzed on his left side. The stroke could not stop Pasteur's fight against disease.

Louis Pasteur with his granddaughter Camille

VACCINES

In 1877, Pasteur began to study **anthrax**, a disease that killed cattle and sheep. He made a weak form of anthrax. It could be given to the animals to protect them. It was called a **vaccine**.

Pasteur now turned his work towards a **rabies** vaccine. Rabies is a disease that kills animals. It can be passed on to people if they are bitten by an animal with rabies.

This cartoon shows a dog with rabies causing panic in London.

In 1884, Pasteur made a rabies vaccine. It helped animals become **immune** to the disease. The next year the vaccine was given to a boy. He had been bitten by a dog with rabies. The boy had to take painful shots, but he never got rabies.

A fifteen-year-old boy is given the rabies vaccine.

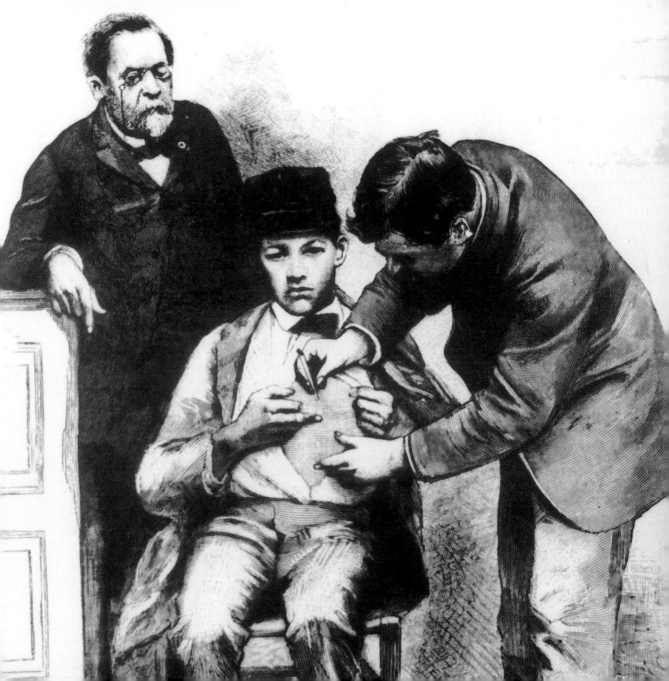

A GREAT SCIENTIST

In 1888, the Pasteur Institute opened in Paris. It is a research and teaching lab for many scientists.

Louis Pasteur died in 1895. He was 72 years old. Pasteur made many important discoveries that helped science and medicine.

Louis Pasteur was the first to work in **microbiology**. His work with microbes later helped scientists and doctors save millions of lives.

Pasteur's work helped doctors and scientists save millions of lives.

PASTEUR

IMPORTANT DATES TO REMEMBER

1822	Born in Dole, France (December 27)
1847	Completes his doctor of science degree
1848	Discovers differences with crystals
1849	Marries Marie Laurent in Strasbourg (May 29)
1865	Experiments with pasteurization
1868	Has first stroke
1881	Anthrax vaccine is a success
1885	Rabies vaccine for humans is a success
1888	Pasteur Institute opens in Paris
1895	Dies (September 28)

GLOSSARY

anthrax (AN thraks) — a disease caused by bacteria that kills cattle and sheep and can be passed on to people

immune (ih MYOON) — protected from a disease

microbes (MY krohb) — tiny living cells, or microorganisms, that can only be seen with a microscope

microbiology (MY kroh by AWL eh jee) — a science about microorganisms, or microscopic life forms

pasteurization (PAS ter eh ZAY shen) — a heating process that kills harmful germs in food, but does not harm the quality of the food

rabies (RAY beez) — a disease in animals caused by a virus that can be given to people through a bite

vaccine (vak SEEN) — a weak form of a virus or microbe that can be given to animals or people to protect them from a disease

yeast (YEEST) — microbes found in sugary liquids that help change the sugar to alcohol

INDEX

Further Reading

Smith, Linda Wasmer. *Louis Pasteur Disease Fighter.* Enslow Publishers, Inc.,1997
Angel, Ann *Louis Pasteur*. Gareth Stevens Childrens Books,1992

Websites To Visit

•www.ambafrance.org/HYPERLAB/PEOPLE/_pasteur.html
•www.labexplorer.com/louis_pasteur.htm

About The Authors

David and Patricia Armentrout specialize in nonfiction writing. They have had several books published for primary school reading. They reside in Cincinnati, Ohio with their two children.